It's a Cow's Life

GREAT STORY & COOL FACTS

Introduction

Welcome to Half and Half books, a great combination of story and facts! You might want to read this book on your own. However, the section with real facts is a little more difficult to read than the story. You might find it helpful to read the facts section with your parent, or someone else, who can help you with the more difficult words. Your parent may also be able to answer any questions you have about the facts—or at least help you find more information!

It's a Cow's Life

English Edition Copyright © 2008 by Treasure Bay, Inc.
English Edition translated by Elizabeth Bell and edited by Sindy McKay

Original edition Copyright © Nathan/VUEF 2003
Original Edition: La vache

Bessie Saves the Day by Laurence Gillot
Illustrated by Lili Scratchy

Non-fiction text by Lucette Brossard
Non-fiction illustrations by Pierre Caillou
Mascot icons by Marc Boutavant

Photography Credits:
Daniel Joubert/REA and Benoît Decout/REA

Special thanks to Margo Souza, Owner & Manager—Circle H Dairy Ranch,
Turlock, CA, for her review and suggestions on the non-fiction
information in this book.

Published by Treasure Bay, Inc.
40 Sir Francis Drake Boulevard
San Anselmo, CA 94960 USA

PRINTED IN SINGAPORE

Library of Congress Catalog Card Number: 2008921429

Hardcover ISBN-13: 978-1-60115-207-7
Paperback ISBN-13: 978-1-60115-208-4

Visit us online at:
www.HalfAndHalfBooks.com

It's a Cow's Life

Table of Contents

Bessie Saves the Day

Story by Laurence Gillot
Illustrated by Lili Scratchy

Nick   Bessie   Nina

One day, my brother Nick and I went to see our grandmother in the hospital.

Grandma was not feeling well. She was not smiling like she usually did. Grandma missed her dear friend, Bessie.

Bessie is a cow.

Grandma said, "Tomorrow is Bessie's birthday." Then she gave us five dollars and told us, "Buy something nice for her."

Nick and I went to the store. We didn't know what a cow would like for a birthday present. Then I had this genius idea!

"Nick! Let's make a party for Bessie!" I said.

Nick liked my genius idea. So we bought birthday candles, balloons, and string. We did not buy a cake, though. Bessie would rather eat grass.

We rushed over to Grandma's farm. Bessie was grazing in the field. We waved at her. Bessie came right over and said "Moo!" She is a very friendly cow. Mooing is how she says hello.

"I wish Grandma could be here for the party, Nina," said Nick.

Then I had my second genius idea. "Let's take the party to Grandma!" I shouted.

Nick was surprised. "You want to take Bessie to the hospital?" he asked.

"Sure!" I said. I told him we could lead her there. We could use his belt for a leash.

Nick smiled and gave me his belt. Holding up his pants with his hand, he asked, "Do you think they will let us in?"

That was a good question.
Then I had my THIRD genius idea.
I told Nick to start blowing up the
balloons.

We tied the balloons to a long string.
We wrapped the string around Bessie.
Soon she was covered in balloons—
horns, hooves, tail, and all!

Now Bessie looked like a
big bunch of colorful balloons.
She looked fantastic!

Everyone smiled at us as we walked by.

The guard at the hospital
did NOT smile at us. He looked
unhappy. "What is that?"
he asked.

"It's just a bunch of birthday
balloons,"I explained.

He nodded and let us in.

Then we saw a nurse coming toward us. She was not smiling either. Her frown made Nick so nervous that he let go of his pants. They fell right down!

The nurse tried hard not to laugh. But she could not help herself. She laughed so hard that she doubled over! Nick and I hurried past her to Grandma's room.

We quickly piled in. The doorway was so small that the balloons started to burst.

POP! POP! POP! POP!

"Nick! Nina! What in the world . . . ?" Grandma began to stammer. Then she saw Bessie. "IT'S MY BESSIE-WESSIE!" she shouted.

Grandma was so happy! She was grinning from ear to ear! Grandma kissed Bessie. Bessie mooed with joy!

The nurse came in. She was frowning again.

But we did not care. We were so happy to see Grandma smiling.

Then I had one more genius idea. I asked Grandma to light the candles. And together we all sang "Happy Birthday" to Bessie!

New Words

graze

Cows pull up grass with their teeth so they can eat it. They walk around and do this all day long.

doubled over

The nurse is laughing so hard she is bent in half at the waist, holding her tummy.

pile in

Everyone goes into the room very fast and all together.

stammer

It is hard for Grandma to speak; her words come out in bits and pieces.

A Cow Family

Barely an hour after it is born, a calf can stand on its own. It nurses for a few months, then starts to graze on grass. It drinks four liters of milk every day for the first month.

A heifer is a young cow that has not yet had calves. It can become a mother once it reaches about two years of age.

Cows and bulls are both cattle. Cows are female. Bulls are males. Cows make milk, but bulls don't. Some cows have horns, and some cows don't have horns.

Bulls are strong and can be dangerous. Never go near a bull in a field.

Modern cattle are descended from the auroch, a wild animal that is now extinct. The auroch was larger than today's cattle. Its horns were more than three feet long.

The Nursing Mom

Milk is a food baby cows cannot do without. It helps them grow. Many people drink cow's milk. They also eat butter, cheese, and yogurt. All of these are made from cow's milk.

To produce milk, a cow must first give birth to a calf. She carries the calf in her belly for nine months. Then her udder fills with milk and she can nurse her baby cow.

Many young calves are sent for a short stay at a special farm just for calves. At the calf farm, they receive special care. They are also given the right amount of milk to help them grow healthy and strong.

Electric milking does not hurt cows.

Cows can be milked two ways: By hand or by an electric milking machine. A cow is milked in the morning and in the evening. She likes to have her leg patted before milking—it makes her feel safe.

A cow can eat about 150 pounds of grass every day. It can also drink more than 20 gallons of water. That's enough water to fill up an entire gas tank of a midsize SUV! A cow stays in the stable in the winter. There it eats a diet of hay and grains such as corn, barley, and oats.

There are many different kinds of cows. Holstein cows came to the U.S. from Holland. They are black and white. They weigh 1,500 pounds when grown up—as much as a small car. They also make the most milk of all the cows.

Grazing on Grass

A cow pulls up grass with a twist of its tongue and swallows it, without chewing, into a pocket called the rumen. Then the cow brings the grass back up into its mouth. It chews the grass again slowly into a mush that is easy to digest. We call this process "chewing the cud."

It has been suggested that cows make better milk when they listen to good music.

A cow speaks. Its deep "moos" are its language for saying things such as "I'm hungry." If another cow cuts in line at feeding time, the cow behind will show anger by butting the line-cutter with its head.

Why does a cow chew its cud? The cow's wild ancestors went through the same double eating process. They were in danger when they grazed in plain view of animals that could prey on them. So they quickly swallowed the grass whole, then took shelter in the forest. Once safe in the forest, they brought the grass back up again and actually chewed it.

Facts about Cows

Every herd of cows has a leader. The leader can make the others obey. She gets to leave the field first. She also goes first to be milked. She is the queen of the herd.

They say the color red makes a bull mad: not true! A bull can see many different colors. But red does not excite bulls any more than green or purple does. When a bull faces a bullfighter, it reacts to the movement of the cape, called a muleta, not to the cape's red color.

Did You Say, "Moo?"

Cows are very social animals. However, a cow may like certain other cows and not like others.

A cow will "moo" and use her face and body to communicate with another cow. What do you think this cow is saying?

Cows give about 6 gallons of milk each day. That's enough for 32 children to have 3 glasses of milk every day!

If you liked *It's a Cow's Life,* here is another Half and Half™ book you are sure to enjoy!

A Doctor for the Animals

STORY: Julie loves all kinds of animals. She loves dogs and cats and horses and fish. One day, she finds a bird that has been hurt. Maybe she can help the bird by taking it to the vet. And maybe, someday, Julie will be a vet herself and help lots of animals.

FACTS: If you like animals, maybe someday you could be a vet! Vets help animals that are sick or hurt. Learn about the different kinds of vets, including city vets, country vets and vets for wild animals! It's all inside and ready for you to explore in this fun-packed book.

To see all the Half and Half books that are available, just go online to **www.HalfAndHalf.com**